# The
# Horrible Holidays

## Audrey Wood

PICTURES BY

## Rosekrans Hoffman

Dial easy-to-read

DIAL BOOKS FOR YOUNG READERS • New York

*For Dean and Kim*
A.W.

*For Elisabeth and Alexander*
R.H.

Published by Dial Books for Young Readers
A Division of Penguin Books USA Inc.
375 Hudson Street
New York, New York 10014

Library of Congress Cataloging in Publication Data
Wood, Audrey. The horrible holidays.
*Summary:* Alf's cousin Mert comes for Christmas
and makes his life horrible.
[1. Cousins—Fiction. 2. Christmas—Fiction.]
I. Hoffman, Rosekrans, ill. II. Title.
PZ7.W846Ho 1988 [E] 87-30617
W
First Hardcover Printing 1988
ISBN 0-8037-0544-1 (tr.)
ISBN 0-8037-0546-8 (lib. bdg.)
3 5 7 9 10 8 6 4 2

First Trade Paperback Printing 1990
ISBN 0-8037-0833-5 (ppr.)
1 3 5 7 9 10 8 6 4 2

The full-color artwork was prepared using pencil,
colored pencils, and colored inks.
It was then scanner-separated and reproduced
as red, blue, yellow, and black halftones.

Reading Level 1.9

# Contents

# THE NO-THANKSGIVING

"Alf!" his mother called.

"They are here!"

Alf put on his plaid coat.

The sleeves were too short.

"Alf!" his father called.

"They've come a long way to see you!"

Alf put on his polka-dot tie.

It looked too long.

"Hey, dude!" his cousin Mert called.

"Come join the party!"

Alf joined the party.

Uncle Hube was playing the piano.

Aunt Ida and Cousin Mert were singing.

"Buffalo gals won't you come out tonight
and dance by the light of the moon."
Everyone clapped loudly.

"Now Alf must sing," said Mert.
Alf tried. "Buffalo gals
won't you dance to the moon."
But the words were wrong.
Everyone clapped loudly anyway.

"Now it's time for card tricks,"
Mert said. "Alf will help.
Pick a card, any card," she said.
Alf picked the queen of hearts.

"Now put it back in the deck,"
said Mert. Alf did as he was told.

"Abracadabra!" Mert cried.

Then she mixed the cards.

"Okay, Alf," Mert said. "Find your card."

Alf looked.

"Wow!" he said. "It's gone!"

"Turn around," Mert said.

"Slowly."

Alf turned around slowly.

"Look!" Aunt Ida cried.

"It's stuck on his behind!"

Alf looked.

The queen of hearts was stuck on his behind.

Mert fell down and laughed.

"That's enough of that," Alf's mother said. "Let's eat Thanksgiving dinner." Everyone sat down.

"First," Alf's father said,

"we should say why we are thankful."

"For health," said Alf's mother.

"For family," said Alf's father.

"For friends," said Aunt Ida.

"For food," said Uncle Hube.

Alf wanted to eat.

But Mert began to read a long,

thankful poem.

The food was getting cold.

At last Mert said,

"It's Alf's turn now."

Alf looked at the cold food.

15

"I don't feel thankful," he said.

"Oh, come now," said his mother.

"You must feel thankful for something."

Alf thought for a moment.

He had to do it.

He picked up Mert's poem.

He stuck it in a glass of water.

"I am thankful," said Alf,

"that Mert does not live in my town."

Alf had to eat Thanksgiving dinner in his room.

# THE CRUMMY CHRISTMAS

It was Christmas Eve.

Cousin Mert, Aunt Ida, and Uncle Hube
were spending the night.

Alf snuck down to the Christmas tree.
He counted his presents.

Just then Mert snuck in.

"You're peeking," she said.

"I'm going to tell."

"I don't peek," said Alf.

"I do," said Mert.

"And I know your presents."

"Don't tell," said Alf.

"I don't want to know."

Mert picked up Alf's biggest present.

"Toot, toot! All aboard, dude!"
she called. Now Alf knew.
It was a train set.

Mert pointed to an odd-shaped present.

"What has four wheels and stripes?"

she asked.

Now Alf knew.

It was a racing car.

Mert picked up a long, thin present.

Alf plugged his ears.

Mert gave it a good swing.

Now Alf knew.

It was a baseball bat.

Alf and Mert snuck back to their rooms.

Mert has ruined everything, Alf thought.

Now I know my presents.

Then Alf remembered.

He had asked for a Spacecraft Radio.

Mert did not know about the radio.

That will be a surprise, Alf thought.

Soon he fell asleep.

The next morning everyone gathered
around the tree.

Alf's father handed out presents.

"What a surprise!" Mert shouted
every time she opened one.

Alf tried to act surprised too.

But he wasn't.

Before long all the presents were opened.

Alf did not get the Spacecraft Radio.

"Everybody happy?" asked Uncle Hube.

Alf was not happy, so he told on Mert.

"Mert just acts surprised," he said.

"She peeked at her presents."

"I never peek at mine," Mert said.

"I only peeked at yours."

Alf's father brought out two
more presents.

"Surprise!" he said.

He handed one to Mert.

The tag on the present read
"To Mert from Cousin Alf."

"I hope it's the Musical Doll
I asked for," Mert said.

Alf's father handed him

the other present.

It said "To Alf from Cousin Mert."

They opened them together.

"Yuck!" cried Mert.

"What is this ugly thing?"

Mert held up a Spacecraft Radio.

"What's this?" Alf said.

He held up a Musical Doll.

Alf looked inside the box.

He found a gold key. Alf wound

the Musical Doll with the gold key.

It played a pretty song.

"It's mine! It's mine!" Mert cried.

"Oops," said Aunt Ida.

"I think there's been a mistake."

Mert tried to grab the Musical Doll.

"Why don't you trade?" said Uncle Hube.

Alf had to do it.

"I like my Musical Doll," he said.

"I think I will keep it.

Thank you, Mert."

"Give it to me!" Mert cried.
"Give it to her!" Alf's mother and
father said. Alf would not give
the Musical Doll to Mert.

Alf spent Christmas morning alone in his room.

# THE UNHAPPY NEW YEAR

It was almost time for the party
to begin.

"I'm sick," Alf said.

"Where?" his mother asked.

"My stomach," Alf said.

"I think I'm dying."

"Maybe it's just gas," his mother said.

Alf flopped on the sofa and
acted sicker.

His mother put him to bed.

*Ding, dong,* the doorbell rang.

"Yoo hoo!" Aunt Ida called.

"Happy New Year!"

"The gang's all here!" Uncle Hube called.

"Where's Alf?"

Alf smiled.

He would not have to join the party.

He would not have to be with Mert.

Soon more guests arrived.

Alf tried to read but the party

was too loud.

Everyone was laughing and singing.

Just then Mert walked in wearing
a silly hat.

*Toweet!*

She blew a horn at Alf.

"Close your eyes," she said.

Alf closed his eyes.

Mert cracked an egg filled with
confetti on Alf's head.

Confetti flew everywhere.

"Too bad you are sick, dude," she said.
Mert blew her horn again, then ran out.

Alf thought about chasing Mert.

He wanted to crack a confetti

egg on her head.

Mert walked back in with a plate

of cake and ice cream.

"Too bad you can't have any, dude,"

she said.

Alf acted like he didn't care.

He pretended to read.

But he saw Mert eat every bite.

"I'll be back," Mert said.

Alf listened to the party.

He heard them play musical chairs and pop-the-balloon.

He heard them shout "Happy New Year!"

Mert walked back in.

"The party's over," she said.

This time Mert handed Alf a present.

"For me?" he said.

Alf opened the present.

It was the Spacecraft Radio.

"Happy New Year," said Mert.

Alf tried to turn the radio on.

But it did not work.

"Too bad I lost the knob," said Mert.

Alf took the Musical Doll from

under his pillow.

"Merry Christmas, Mert," he said.

"Wow, thanks!" said Mert.

"I will play it every night before
I go to sleep."

"Mert!" Uncle Hube called.

"Let's go home!"

Alf watched them drive away.

Then he reached into his pocket.

He took out the gold key.

"See you next year, dude," he said

with a smile.

At last Alf rolled over and fell asleep.